counting christmas

counting christmas

by karen katz

*

MARGARET K. McELDERRY BOOKS
NEW YORK LONDON TORONTO SYDNEY SINGAPORE

ten

tiny lights get twirled
around the tree.

10

nine shiny presents are wrapped

so prettily.

9

eight

cookies for Santa
baked by little elves.

seven velvet stockings hang

above the hearth.

six

slippered feet race
upstairs to bed.

five
Christmas stars hang over drowsy heads.

✳ ✳ ✳ ✳ ✳

four

loving arms wrap
hugs around each child.

❋ ❋ ❋ ❋

4

three sleeping children dream

of treats and toys. ✳ ✳ ✳ 3

two silver bells jingle on

Santa's sleigh. ❄ ❄ 2

one magical day for families and

children to share. ✳ **1**

To all the children in the world, especially Lena Zuli
Special thanks to Emma

Margaret K. McElderry Books
An imprint of Simon & Schuster Children's
Publishing Division
1230 Avenue of the Americas
New York, NY 10020

Book design by Daniel Roode
The text of this book is set in Venetian.
The illustrations are rendered in collage,
gouache, and colored pencils.

Manufactured in China
10 9 8 7 6 5 4 3 2 1
Library of Congress Cataloging-in-Publication Data
Katz, Karen.
Counting Christmas / Karen Katz.— 1st ed.
p. cm.
Summary: Three children getting ready for Christmas
count down from ten to one in anticipation of Christmas
morning.
ISBN 0-689-84925-7 (hardcover)
[1. Christmas—Fiction. 2. Counting.] I. Title.
PZ7.K15745 Cp 2003
[E]—dc21
2002009783